WOULD A FROG EAT A FIG?

Written by
Cheryl Mc Ryan

Illustrated by Ana Rankovic

For Lauren, Nick, and Jenna

First edition published 2019
ISBN 978-1-7336769-0-8

Have you ever wondered about
the foods people eat?

Where they live can decide
their most treasured treat.

Animals are the same
—they eat what they find.

If offered something different,
do you think they would mind?

Anteaters love Ants,
this we all know.
But would they eat
Apricots tied with a bow?

Aa

Buffalos might nosh on a Bowl full of Berries.

Bb

Cc

Would a Cheetah eat Cake filled with red Cherries?

Dd

Of course, Dogs
want Donuts and
even chew shoes.

Yet give an Emu
an Egg and it'll be
singing the blues.

Ee

Would a Frog choose a Fig over a buzzing Fly?

Ff

Gg

Or a Gorilla eat Guava
while wearing a tie?

Hamsters would delight
in sweet Honeydew.

Hh

But I've never seen an Iguana in an Ice cream queue.

Ii

A Jaguar just might
give Jackfruit the boot.

Jj

Kk

And Kangaroos would ditch Kiwi for fresh veggie root.

Ll

Ladybugs eat Leaves
or an occasional mite.

Mm

Would Meerkats
eat Mangoes 'til
the very last bite?

Nn

Newts look for worms;
Nuts aren't their wish.

Oo

Would Otters try Oranges
after eating fresh fish?

Pp

Pythons put the squeeze on Parsnip and Peach.

Qq

Yet for Quail, a Quince is Quite out of reach.

Rr

Roosters like Raspberries,
or at least I think they do.

Ss

Seals love Sardines
and I KNOW this is true.

Tt

For a Turtle, some Turnips are a real delight.

Uu

Udon for Umbrellabirds
is a reason for flight.

Vv

A Viper won't eat
Veggies no matter
the day.

Ww

If a Warthog finds
Wasabi will it leave
it or stay?

Xx

X marks the spot
of the X-ray tetra.
It won't eat a Xigua
even if there is extra.

Yy

Yaks might try a Yam
if given a chance.

Zz

And Zucchini
for Zebras is
a reason
to prance.

Some animals in this book are on the threatened
or endangered list, which means they are at risk
of remaining a healthy animal population.
Reasons for endangerment can be loss of habitat
(where they find their food), hunting, or diseases.
To find out more about the amazing animals
in our world visit World Wildlife Fund at:
www.worldwildlife.org

CPSIA information can be obtained at www.ICGtesting.com
Printed in the USA
BVIW120131230919
559083BV00038BA/643

9 781733 676908